Heads I Win, Tails You Lose

Linda Hutsell-Manning

AOS Publishing, 2024

Linda Hutsell-Manning

ISBN: 978-1-990496-26-4

Cover Design: Chanelle Poupart

Visit AOS Publishing's website:
www.aospublishing.com

I

What Anne notices first are the two little piles of dust and, an instant later, the empty wheelchair footrests. She blinks thinking she must be seeing things, assuming to see what should be there, Harold's wrinkled feet, yellowed toenails. Her head is under the table, bending down to pick up the teaspoon she dropped when he jerked his arm again, all the while listening to him mumble it was an accident, certain he is frowning, one black eyebrow raised, piercing blue eyes fixed on her.

He's in one of his moods this morning, she thinks numbly. Another long weekend ahead.

"Hurry up, will you Anne, my feet are cold."

Anne bangs her head on the kitchen table as she stands up.

"You almost spilled the milk."

"Sorry. Do you want the rest of your cereal?"

"I told you my feet are cold."

"I'll get your socks."

"And my slippers."

Anne leans against the bedroom dresser, sweat running down between her shoulder blades. Morning sun pours in, zig-zagging a crazy design on the delicately patterned wallpaper. Less than an hour ago, she lifted those lifeless feet squarely onto the footrests and noticed his toenails needed cutting.

You're in overload, she says to herself, pulling open the dresser drawer and yanking out a clean pair of socks. Things have been hectic all week at the Library and she hasn't had time to recover. She grabs his plaid slippers from under the bed and hurries back to the kitchen.

The clock ticks out of sync with Harold's raspy breathing. When Anne arrived home Friday, Mrs. Forester, the housekeeper, beckoned Anne outside saying hurriedly that Harold's breathing had been increasingly rough the last couple of days. Anne hopes they're not in for another bout of pneumonia.

"My Corn Pops are all mushy now," Harold snaps, "What took you so long?"

Anne inhales sharply. She thinks of slamming the slippers down on the table beside him but doesn't. She maneuvers the wheelchair back and toward her. Harold's legs, covered with a wool blanket, hang passively in front. She's sure, now, she imagined it.

She hasn't.

Where his feet were, less than an hour ago, nothing. She lifts one pant leg to find the bottom of his ankle curved round, the skin taut and shiny. Shaking, she tries to pull the socks over each stump until she stops, gagging involuntarily.

"My slippers," he reminds her, "When Mrs. Forester is here, she always puts them on before breakfast."

"I didn't notice holes in these socks," she manages to say, snatching them up. "I'll get another pair."

"Well hurry, will you, my feet are like ice."

Back in the bedroom, she sits on the bed and tries to stop shaking; wonders if she's becoming delusional. As if it were yesterday, she remembers a particular Psychology class, all of them keen and much too arrogant, the professor talking about after-effects of unexpected trauma, how the mind in a state of disbelief uses coping mechanisms one of which is to simply go along with the situation as if it were perfectly normal. She stands numbly and opens the dresser drawer. Another memory follows, a first aid course she took a couple of years ago where the instructor said amputees frequently have feeling in a missing limb. Steadying herself momentarily against the dresser drawer, she stuffs each sock with three other pairs.

Harold glowers when she returns to the kitchen. "I've changed my mind," he says, "I want toast."

"First things first," she says brightly, reaching down to pull on the socks. "This will only take a minute." Even though scrunching the socks into the slippers is tricky, the final result seems quite respectable. She feels like some other version of herself, tougher, unexpectedly resilient.

While making toast at the counter, she again eyes the two little piles of dust under the table. They look harmless enough, like something accidentally spilled. Sand from down at the beach perhaps.

"Isn't it almost time for Oprah?" Harold asks. "Mrs. Forester always..."

"It's Saturday morning, Harold, there's nothing on but cartoons."

"Well hurry up, I'm probably missing the best ones."

Anne watches the back of his head in front of the blaring TV. Today Harold's feet are the least of her worries. She's not going to start feeling sorry for herself, for her life and what it's come to, there simply isn't time. Laundry first, then a dinner party to plan. This month it's her turn.

Harold's university colleagues have been more than generous since his car accident, a head-on collision coming around the curve. Three teens in a small sedan dead by the time anyone arrived at the scene, scattered like tossed luggage outside the vehicle. The Audi Sport had good air bags, resilient frame, otherwise it would have been four dead.

For the past year and a half, almost everyone in several departments have gathered for a monthly soireé, an event. Harold who had, and has, a wide circle of interesting and influential friends at the University, lives for these events. Conversation is always exhilarating. Post supper, after more than a few drinks and toasts, they all settle in to argue, josh, cajole. Harold has always been a great raconteur, a centre stage man, and the old spark still draws them in. It's the only time he's close to being himself again.

Last month's party was at the Runston's, a huge old Victorian-looking place on the edge of town, laughter and conversation in the large resplendent living room, guests spilling out onto the stone balcony, the smell of sea air drifting in.

"He should write a book," Mavis Hilliard said, out in the kitchen where they were getting more Scotch and Vodka.

"Oh, he's already doing that," Anne replied. "He's been dictating into a tape recorder."

"How fascinating..."

Anne eased herself away from Mavis as quickly as possible. Mavis's husband was Department Head and she used her cut throat curiosity to advantage whenever she could. Anne was not in the mood for dissection.

"Good old Harold," George Hanson broke in, taking the Scotch bottle from Anne, "Remember the time he..."

Anne excused herself and retreated to the washroom. The party was in full swing and she needed a break. Not that she didn't like these parties, but she had to be careful - even a short animated discussion with any given husband could be misconstrued. After all, she did have an invalid spouse. Even though she would have loved to participate in some of the discussions; comment on arguments she knew were faulty, she had learned to stay quietly behind her bookish librarian mask. It was safer that way.

Anne puts a dark load of wash in first because of Harold's black socks. He insists on dressing to the nines for these affairs. It's his old tux now - ever since he rediscovered The Great Gatsby. After demanding the DVD four or five times in a row, Anne threatened to hide it.

"That's the trouble with you," he whined, "no tolerance. No appreciation of real discovery. I'm analyzing it. May even do a paper."

"On the movie?"

"Of course not. On Fitzgerald. I'd forgotten how fascinating he is."

It wasn't worth arguing about. He would get onto something and flog it to death, way beyond death. She refused *to fall for his bait. They always ended up in a shouting match and Harold would win by having a violent coughing attack.*

She looks at the clock. "I have to go into town," she calls, "a bunch of things to do for the party."

"How long will you be gone?"

"Half an hour, an hour, I'm not sure."

"Time means so little to you. You squander it. Throw it away."

"Harold, I have to go to the cleaners, the post office, the meat market, probably the supermarket..."

Why does she always do this? Explain herself to him like a child. Justify everything.

"Put the timer on please."

She takes the timer from the shelf; winds it viciously back to its one hour limit and sets it ticking.

"One hour," he says, emphasizing it.

"I may be longer."

The laneway is brimming over with sun and warm breezes; bougainvillea splash colour against the faded stucco house; the smell of sea water from the Bay pungent even from here. She climbs into the old Chevy van and is relieved it starts without a hitch. Friends tease Harold about its age. "You know you could afford another second vehicle. Something better for Anne," Fred Aldershaft always says. "Get a used sports car. You owe it to her, for God's sakes." Harold always laughs it off, makes some comment about what's really important in life. It doesn't matter to him and the van is equipped with a wheelchair lift. Anne would love a small red Honda. Her library salary is less than half what Harold made and his disability pension is less than his teaching salary; adequate, but it doesn't leave much leeway with all the added day-to-day expenses, especially not for large ticket items. She does have her own savings but they're off limits, waiting for some extraordinary moment, some unforeseen turn in her life.

The van creaks and rattles down the bumpy gravel roadway, this so familiar route, everything tinged with her numbness, her need to concentrate only on the task at hand. The drive into town takes less than twenty minutes and, normally, she'd walk or ride her bike, but today there are too many cumbersome things to carry back. Even with the van windows closed and the engine humming, she still hears the infernal timer.

The timer was Mrs. Forester's idea. Dear Mrs. Forester - housekeeper, nursemaid. What would Anne do without her? "Let's see how long it takes to eat our lunch," she always crooned. "Ready now, here we go." She uses the timer like a kindergarten game. Anne thought Harold would be insulted but he wasn't. He seems to revel in it. Mrs. Forester is never ruffled; she takes everything in her stride as Harold is always reminding Anne. "Why don't you do it like Mrs. Forester?" She treats him like an indulgent child and he laps it up - from the chocolate chip cookies to those ridiculous bow ties she gives him at Christmas and his birthday. The one from this past Christmas had lights and a battery and Harold insisted on wearing it every day for two weeks. She also talks baby talk to him - Anne has overheard her, a number of times. It's as if the two of them have a secret relationship during the day when she is gone, little tete-a-tetes and routines encompassing so many of the things she thought Harold detested and looked down on. He behaves like a school boy playing hooky. It appalled Anne at first. Harold was always so particular, so arrogantly immaculate. She couldn't imagine him this way but then she hadn't imagined a head-on collision.

Early spring two years ago, late evening, rain pelting against the patio doors. Harold was working late with one of his grad students at the university. When the phone rang she almost didn't hear it, fire crackling, Andrea Bocelli singing Puccini.

"Mrs. Dexter? There's been an accident. Your husband is on his way to City View Hospital."

"Is he badly hurt?"

"Can you meet us there?"

"Yes, of course. What happened?"

"Head-on collision. High Bay Parkway."

Conversation muffled, only a few words audible: "Oxygen, heart- rate, blood..." Connection gone.

Anne barely remembers the drive: pelting rain, bad visibility, too many red lights. Harold, her clever, polite, gregarious Harold lay unconscious, bandaged and tubed, plugged into too many machines, all of them ticking, flashing, monitoring. She must have looked pale. A nurse took her arm while someone pushed a chair against her knees. She collapsed into it close to the bed. One of Harold's hands lay outside the blanket, his neatly trimmed nails the only concrete evidence of his presence. She laid her hand carefully over his, shocked to feel how cold it was, almost lifeless.

She spent the night there, numb and disbelieving, nurses and doctors slipping in and out, checking, whispering, almost as if she didn't exist.

Once or twice when she tried to ask a question; get someone's attention, one of them would murmur, "Too soon, Mrs. Dexter. Ask in the morning."

Morning stretched to days, weeks, months and into another year. For the first month, she went directly from work, taking short breaks for some hospital fast food, sitting zombie-like beside the bed, her head playing out dozens of plausible and unplausible scenarios while, at the same time, fiercely hoping for a miracle. Twenty-seven days after the accident, Harold gained consciousness, blinked his eyes, squeezed her hand. For the next few weeks, she was giddy with hope.

Three young idiots drunk and reckless, no seatbelts on. Cannon fodder, Harold called them later that month when he was finally able to mumble a few words.

Full speech returned, occasionally the twinkle in his eye but never, now, for her. His congenial polite self was as silent as his lifeless body, immobilized from the neck down. He seemed grateful at first, then morose and finally bitter. Harold stripped taut into someone else, someone demanding, cold and self-absorbed.

Heroic was what her colleagues at the library called her. "How is he doing today?" they kept asking during those first awful months when she spent every evening at the hospital. She was numb, removed from herself, an observer of what everyone told her was her life. Sometime during the third month, he had regained a little feeling in one leg and, for a short time, she went around with the impossible hope that everything would return to what it had been. Harold would teach his English courses and work with his grad students; they would have long, intense discussions about books they both read; make gourmet meals once a month; canoe or ski on weekends and, occasionally, make love. Sensuality had never been one of Harold's strong points and Anne was too shy to initiate, even after twelve years of marriage.

After six months in the hospital, the doctors confirmed what she already knew. He was, and would forever be, a quadriplegic.

The house was redesigned for wheelchair accessibility: a ramp up to the front door, several doorways widened, custom doors installed, the bathroom redesigned. Anne found this intrusion into her life difficult. She was, by nature, more reclusive than Harold and their home was private, entered only by invitation. Carpenters, electricians, plumbers, building inspectors - she felt set adrift, an alien in her own house.

Gradually, over the last year, when she realized it would always be like this - that there would be weekly visits by nurses, social workers, physiotherapists - she transferred her more private things to the library. She reorganized a storage room adjacent to her office and, after removing most of the accumulated library clutter, found a surplus desk, lamp and an old leather couch. After the night cleaners gave it a good vacuuming, she organized the furniture and brought in a collection of favourite books, all her journals, an old CD player and gradually most of their CDs. Harold wasn't much interested in music anymore, preferring TV, game shows and soaps. She retreated there to save her sanity, recreate a memory, ballast against the impossibility of how things had turned out. Occasionally, she'd stay all night; make last minute arrangements with Mrs. Forester; say she had a report to finish and she had no idea how long it would take. She would read, write in her journal, drink some wine and pretend she was someone else.

"What do you do all evening when you're there?" Harold whined, early in January, after she'd stayed away twice in one week.

"You know what I do - work on reports, fill out all those damn statistical surveys they're always sending around."

"You really expect me to believe that?"

"What else would I be doing?"

"I'm not naive, Anne, I can see it."

"See it? See what?"

"Myself as the cuckold."

"That's ridiculous." Anne felt her cheeks burning. The accusation was more than ridiculous. When would she have time?

"I'm offended, I really am. I don't know how you could..."

Harold closed his eyes and hummed. It was his way of saying the conversation was over, the issue closed.

He could hum indefinitely; she always ran out of words.

A pattern developed. For a while, the days passed routinely. She would bend over backwards to be kind, sympathetic. This always worked for a few months, then something would happen at work - a deadline, a ministry report and she would have to work late a few days in a row. Harold would become increasingly testy - she would snap back - Mrs. Forester would coddle more, then an out and out fight.

They often argued before the accident but never, in her memory, had they shouted at each other. Arguments, then, always ended in some kind of consensus, not a direct truce perhaps, but by one of them subtly changing the subject or asking an unrelated question. Now fangs were bared and nothing was resolved. She wished she could talk to someone about it. She didn't know anyone at the library that well; her university friends were all busy with their own lives, and her parents? She couldn't possibly say anything to her parents. Her mother called every Sunday evening, asking how she was doing, how Harold was feeling. She knew they desperately wanted everything to be all right, for their daughter's life to return to the idyllic state they perceived it had been. She made things up to make them feel better. Yes, Harold seemed a little brighter some days; make it all sound as normal as possible. She knew she was convincing herself as much as placating them.

This past winter was particularly difficult. Harold had been admitted to hospital twice with pneumonia, emaciated, wheezy, morose. There were days when her flesh crawled at the thought of touching him. Then guilt would consume her and she would spend more time preparing his favourite dishes; buy him some new clothes. She tried to imagine what it must be like trapped and unable to do anything but think and dream. She wondered if he did dream any more. She wondered so many things but when she tried to ask him he always cut her off short, made her feel insignificant.

He had always been the dominant one in their relationship but before it was generous and politely caring. Ten years her senior, her English professor and mentor, their relationship had begun when she was an undergrad - long discussions in his office over some point in one of her essays. She stood up for herself in those days, held her own when he tried to insist she was wrong.

She remembers being furious when he redlined her comment that a character "donned a role", even put a minus two beside the phrase. She stormed into his office and slapped her essay on his desk.

He looked up, as if mildly amused. "How delightful to see you again. Your essay was excellent, I don't usually give marks that high."

She stayed standing, knowing from Psych class that this gave her the dominant stance. "I don't understand," she began, "why you objected to my use of the word don."

"Sit down," he said, gesturing to the chair beside her, waiting until she did before continuing. "If my memory serves me correctly, one can only don a piece of clothing."

"I meant figuratively," she said, leaning forward, "that this character donned a role as one would a cloak."

"Ah, as in fiction," he added looking more bemused.

"This is fiction that I'm writing about." She tapped the paper with her finger. "I assumed you would understand this, that he donned the role as one would a cloak."

Professor Dexter pulled down a copy of Oxford Concise Dictionary and read out to her. "To don - put on an item of clothing."

"I know that," she said, a little derisively. "I was simply extending it, being creative in my thinking."

He leaned forward and met her gaze.

She found him mildly attractive, his tweed jacket, turtleneck, elegant sideburns. "And do you think, Miss Harrison, that there is room for this kind of creativity in standard essay form?"

"There is in my essay form," she replied.

"I can't give you a higher mark."

"I don't want a higher mark. I simply want you to tell me my use of this word in this sentence..." She tapped the paper again. "...is not wrong.

"I will contend that you have a convincing argument."

"A valid argument?"

"I think we should agree to disagree and leave it at that."

It was the beginning of many such interesting encounters. He was unbelievably old school from Anne's point of view; she felt it her duty to shake him up a little.

Some Profs discussed student essays over coffee. She wouldn't have minded this, being often sleep deprived when she went to see him but she wouldn't dream of suggesting it. One professor even held his classes in the Campus pub. Anne wouldn't take his course for that very reason. She thought it sensationalistic and a bit crass. She knew it was verboten, profs dating students; knew this prof had a reputation; bent the rules and got away with it.

She had only dated a couple of times in university and never in high school. She was a proverbial wall flower, bookish. All clichés applied: an only child in a structured household, her mother a retired concert pianist who taught from home, her father a tax accountant, long office hours, proper and somewhat distant. She had her choice of three universities and, having never gone anywhere on her own before, chose the one in her own province, albeit not in Vancouver where her parents lived, but in Victoria. Her mother's parents lived there and they visited often when she was a child. She adored the hour and a half ferry ride and, finding the University of Victoria had a reputable English Department, chose it over the other two. Her mother insisted she try living in residence, said it was one of those necessary rites of passage. She lasted until Thanksgiving weekend. The constant noise drove her crazy: she couldn't concentrate, her roommate did nothing but paint her nails and play loud unrecognizable music, and there was no privacy, always someone dropping in or a crowd out in the hall, on weekends parties that lasted all night. After the first month, she called home every evening begging for a place of her own and finally just before Thanksgiving, her parents found her a small apartment off campus. Money was not an issue, and she kept the same second floor flat for her four undergrad years, staying on over the summers tutoring students who had failed Intro English and were required to take a make-up course. She was good at this and had a waiting list of interested clients.

Throughout her four years, majoring in English, writing and pushing her idea of form and style whenever she could, she thought little of her discussions with Professor Dexter other than they were interesting, stimulating. It never occurred to her he might find her attractive. His lectures were spellbinding and she managed to take all the courses he taught.

At her graduation ceremony, it was he who presented her with her Arts degree Cum Laude. "I am so proud of you," he whispered, giving her hand a squeeze. She nodded; felt her neck redden. Her hand remembered his right through her mother fussing with her hair, her dad taking pictures, small sandwiches, petite fours and too many people milling everywhere. No one except her parents had previously taken interest in her academic achievements. The afternoon was charged with proud parents and preening grads. Her parents were too reserved to say much and she felt, standing in this crowd of ebullience and celebration, an enormous sense of loss, of being set adrift. Even though she knew she'd been accepted at Library School, she had the feeling order was falling away, parameters gone. She suddenly wanted to chat with Professor Dexter one more time and wandered around pretending to look for other classmates but he had left or didn't stay for the niceties.

II

It wasn't until late that fall, when she was fully immersed in courses at UBC Library School, that she was called into the reception office and handed a sealed envelope by the secretary.

"Someone who must want to get in touch with you," the woman said, smiling. "Your Alma Mater insignia on the envelope?"

Anne nodded, wondering who it could possibly be. She took the envelope and hurried out, sitting on the nearest bench to read the letter. Professor Dexter had tracked her down through the university office and wondered if he could take her out to dinner. She put the letter down, flabbergasted. Dinner with Professor Dexter? What would they talk about? She was no longer an English major. Many of her courses were boring and geared to library administration. She read on. He had a meeting at her university in two weeks and didn't have to teach until the next day.

Back at her apartment, she called the number he provided, leaving a message on his answering service. His phone message was abrupt and to the point. So like him, she thought, hanging up. This should be interesting.

Meeting him again was as if no time had lapsed, like a brief pause between sentences.

"Anne," he said, taking her hand in both of his. "I'm so pleased you agreed to this." They were on the steps of the library, early evening, a scented breeze blowing from somewhere. "I'm sure you're busy with all your courses."

"A surprise hearing from you," Anne began, leaving her hand in his a moment longer than she should have, feeling red rising up her pale neck. Like a damn teenager she thought, pulling away to flip her hair forward, hoping it didn't show.

"You must call me Harold," he said gesturing down the steps. "My car is close by and I've booked us into a small place, a favourite of mine."

She nodded and they walked in silence. She could think of nothing to say, and he obviously didn't think conversation necessary.

The restaurant was elegant and not the kind she would have gone to with any of her university friends. They sat in a secluded spot on a large, covered porch that overlooked the ocean, the sun orange and brimming its last rays into the distant horizon. As it was midweek and past tourist season, only one other couple was there when they arrived and, by the time they finished their entree, they were alone. Once the light lessened, the waitress came with two candles, their flames highlighting the silver cutlery and better than average restaurant china. Anne basked in the elegance of it all and wondered what the evening had in store. Their conversation turned out to be typically professor/student driven, he asking specific questions, she answering: her courses, profs, several of whom he knew, how she compared this university to her Alma Mater.

"And your plans after graduation?"

"I haven't given it much thought yet."

"A PhD program perhaps?"

"No, I'll have had enough of school after these next two semesters. I'll start applying for library jobs, I suppose. Maybe travel a little."

He said nothing and stared out the window. She wondered if he thought her unambitious but felt flattered he had suggested post grad work.

Afterward, he drove her to her apartment and walking her up the outside stairs to her door, bid her a courteous goodnight. He didn't mention another meeting or comment positively about their extended table discussions. Well, she thought to herself, as she locked the door and took off her shoes, I guess that was that.

Until he called again.

Even though it was over a three-hour drive between campuses, he insisted on meeting her once a month that fall and winter, late Friday afternoons saying he liked the ferry ride over, that it gave him a chance to read and make notes for next week's classes. They would have dinner and then discuss literary and academic points long into the night: in cafes, on park benches and, eventually, in her small apartment. She wondered if he would want to bed her and decided, after several sleepless nights going over pros and cons, that she would go for it, that he obviously wanted her in his life and even though he didn't say so, that it would be worth it. She made sure her sheets were always clean on days when they were meeting, even made a conscious effort at flirting but with no experience and less confidence, she was sure he didn't notice.

One rainy spring evening, after a more sumptuous dinner than usual, he ordered Champagne and insisted they toast to her future, her becoming a librarian and finally, to her as the most beautiful and intelligent woman he had ever met. She balked at this last toast, held her glass at bay staring hard at him. Did he mean he loved her? Was he leading up to something?

He put his glass down and solemnly pulled a small box from his jacket pocket. She took it gingerly, sensing a moment approaching, as if she were reading a novel and knew though wasn't admitting what was to come on the next page.

As she slowly opened the box, he said in a husky voice not at all his own, "Anne will you marry me?"

The ring was magnificent, a large solitary diamond in a discreet white gold setting. She nodded as he slipped the ring on her wedding finger. They drank the rest of the Champagne and returned to her apartment. Once in the car, however, he seemed to forget what had just transpired and started into a lively discussion on the merits and demerits of modern poetry. Anne still overcome by the ring on her finger, her instant response to his request for marriage, the implications of it all, found it difficult to concentrate on what he was saying. She surfaced only when his intellectual tirade against the validity of modern writing in general reached supercilious proportions, at which point she began countering with all her intellectual strength, in its defense so that by the time they were up the stairs and into her apartment she was almost ready to give him back the ring. When he realized he was pushing it too far, he recanted somewhat and steered the conversation in another direction.

Sometime after midnight, when they were making a snack in the kitchen, he ran his hand over her long silky hair to her breasts and around onto her trim buttocks. "You are so enticing," he murmured, "but we must wait." She nodded and cut several more pieces of Camembert on two individual plates. His caress gave her a slight tingly feeling, nothing more and as she had no previous experience, thought this reaction to be perfectly normal.

"We'll make our wedding plans," he said, bidding her goodnight with his usual cursory kiss. "I'll give you a call tomorrow. "Will you be in late afternoon?"

Anne nodded and closed the door, listening to his footsteps fade down the stairwell. She sat for a long time on the couch in the unlit room, looking at the stars through her living room window, occasionally glancing at the ring fragmenting their glow. In novels, especially the eighteenth and nineteenth century ones, heroines always "basked in radiance" after a marriage proposal. She tried to analyze what she was feeling. Surprised and flattered were the only two adjectives she could conjure up. Her parents would be ecstatic especially her mother who was always fishing for possibilities in her personal life. She had only briefly mentioned Professor Dexter, that they met occasionally to discuss one or more of her courses, that she saw him as her mentor, never that they went dinner, never that he came to her apartment. Compared to everything she had read about men in general, she was amazed by his sexual reserve, continually expecting that at some undefined moment he would become the proverbial predator forcing his sexual attentions on her. She did know he came from a strict Presbyterian family who enforced rules and repression. Not unlike her own, without the religion.

She stood up and twirled around in a circle leading with her left hand. She was engaged to Professor Harold Dexter; her future was secure. Why question his reserve?

They married less than a month after her graduation, a ceremony at Fair Weather Presbyterian Church in Vancouver, his parent's church. The ceremony, rather stiff and formal, was extremely brief. A friend from her undergrad days, Susie Ainsworth was her Maid of Honour. Susie was finishing her Masters and heading into a PhD program. Before the wedding, she railed at Anne several times about throwing her life away and wasting her intellect. "He's too old for you," was one of her favourite lines. "Just think, when you're in your fifties and still raring to go, he'll be thinking about retirement." Susie turned out to be suitably demure at the wedding, however, chatting affably with parents and older relatives, taking the church hall sandwiches and tea reception in her stride.

Anne, who was mingling at the reception, watched Harold's elderly mother hanging on her son's arm beaming at everyone, her own parents trying to fit into these alien surroundings. They were used to cocktails before supper, wine with every meal. Anne still remembers watching them all waving as they drove off to a hotel, to the beginning of her new life.

Their wedding night was not memorable. It wasn't as if she didn't know what was going to happen, just not how quickly it would be over... how painful those brief moments would be.

Harold fell asleep immediately while she tiptoed to the bathroom to repair the damages. The strap of her negligee was loose and she wet and sticky. She lay awake for some time, afterward, thinking how different this was from any written descriptions of sex she had read in novels.

They spent almost two months in England, an extended honeymoon, visiting countless cathedrals, palaces and writers' birth places: Wordsworth's dark cottage, the home of the Bronte sisters on the bleak Yorkshire moors, Shakespeare's birthplace on Henley Street in Stratford-upon-Avon. She was especially taken with Blenheim Palace in Oxfordshire and the turbulent life of Consuelo Vanderbilt who became through her mother's bullying the Duchess of Marlborough, thus linked in marriage and social status to the prestigious Churchill family. That evening, Anne argued vociferously with Harold about arranged marriages and the superficiality of the aristocracy. Harold took it all as a verbal sparring match and, when things came to close to becoming nasty, he defused the situation as if it were some heated discussion in one of his classes. Anne, tired by this time, simply gave in. It was a pattern that repeated itself a number of times during their honeymoon.

Mostly however every day was an adventure, evening discussions entertaining, sex an occasional after-thought. It seemed normal to her, and she was relieved that sex, being the messy business it was, was thankfully not one of Harold's priorities. English history on the other hand, excited and enthralled them both. Harold was so knowledgeable, often adding comments to a given guide's commentary, occasionally tripping one up with a correction.

Anne accepted this, absorbed every day and recorded much of it in a journal she brought especially for the trip, an exquisite leather-bound notebook she had found several years ago in a specialty shop in Victoria. It had an amber stone embedded in its cover surrounded by two rows of elaborate stitching, hand pressed paper thick and luxurious to the touch.

She had saved it for some special occasion, and this seemed to be it. Harold raised his eyebrows when she crammed it into her carry on.

"Won't you find that a tad heavy to lug around England?" he said. He was sorting ties, deciding which six he would put into his slim traveling suitcase.

"I don't think so," she replied, winding its leather cord around to hold the pages in place. "I plan to sit by windows and record everything. I may want to write on the plane."

"There'll be plenty of time," Harold said, looking mildly amused. "It's a five-hour flight."

During evenings she wrote in a fine even hand, sometimes before supper, sometimes afterward. Harold often went down to the bar to find someone to regale with, more than one usually ending up at their table. She always felt redundant and, after a few episodes of listening for an hour or two in crowded pubs with excessive noise and bad music, she excused herself before he even suggested she come along; said she wanted to study their latest purchased book. By the end of the trip three quarters of the journal pages were filled. She did read from the accumulating book collection they had bought: art books, travel books, a few rare editions from quaint little second hand book stores. So many that in the end Harold had to ship them home separately.

Contrary to what her friend Susie predicted, she found it delightful returning to Harold's already established home close to Victoria off the Cassandra Bay Road. She had only been there once, a week before their wedding, a hurried trip to deposit her belongings in his house. Harold had hired two of his grad students to do the work at both ends. Her mother, so taken with this unexpected good fortune in her daughter's life, stood the doorway saying "Oh my, oh my" over and over as boxes, clothes and books were carried out.

Once back at his house, Harold insisted she find a place for most of her things: clothes in the closet, books on bookshelves, dishes and kitchen utensils tucked away. She marveled he had already made room for her, emptied shelves waiting and ready. There was no time then to walk down to the Bay although he did point out the partly overgrown trail leading to it when he took her out on the cedar deck overlooking the lawn and trees beyond. For the first few weeks after they returned, she felt as if she were still on holiday in some elegant country house and was continually surprised to find her own belongings already there. She settled in effortlessly, pleased that life according to Harold had begun.

Susie, and a few other university friends she still kept in touch with, chided her for letting Harold make all the decisions. "You'll regret it," they told her. "At some point you'll want your freedom back." She argued she had no interest in day-to-day mundanities, that she couldn't care less. Her life with Harold was satisfying, steady and immeasurably pleasant.

In those first few months, Anne was continually amazed by Harold's vast experience and knowledge; the connections he seemed to have everywhere. She had been checking library positions online and had already filled out several basic application forms when he arrived home one evening to announce he had arranged for her to have an interview, a library position in the town close to his home. She had never gone through a real job interview and was terrified at the thought of this one. In high school, her father had always talked to some local employer who was more than pleased to take her on for the summer. That her father was this man's tax accountant probably factored largely in the equation. Nearing the end of her first year in university, the English Department Head, impressed with her marks and ability to sustain an effective argument, offered her the tutoring job.

"I don't have much experience with interviews," she said, staring at him across the big oak table after supper. "What am I supposed to say?"

"Just be your charming self," Harold replied, raising his glass to her. "I'm sure it won't be a problem."

And it wasn't. It was as if she already had the job when she went for the interview. The Library Board members said her credentials were exemplary and that Professor Dexter and several of his university staff had highly recommended her. A very pregnant young librarian stayed on the first month, easing her into her myriad of responsibilities. Near the end of the first year, when this librarian's Maternity leave was ending, the Senior Library Assistant announced her husband had taken a position in another province and they would be leaving. Anne applied and was given the position. Her life seemed to be on an even keel, slipping effortlessly from student to interim Librarian to her current full-time position. She loved this small-town library and if once in a while she longed for something more exciting, something a tad dangerous, she would read a good novel and imagine herself the protagonist. Everyone kept telling her how fortunate she was. Secure with an intelligent, handsome husband. What else could she ask for?

III

Anne parks the car down by the old fish warehouse. It's not used anymore and there's talk of the Yacht Club buying the property. It would be a shame in a way. She loves the rundown wildness of it, the building leaning tiredly toward the water as if, perhaps, ready to disappear. She always listens to waves lap against its darkened wooden dock before walking back up to Main Street. First stop, the meat market. A keen new couple have taken over and expanded the deli section with a number of gourmet salads and cheeses.

"And how are you this fine morning, Mrs. Dexter?"

"I'm hosting our monthly get together," Anne says, "so I'm feeling a little stressed."

"You'll be wanting cold cuts and an assortment from the deli counter?"

She nods. "You decide for me," she says. There will be about twenty people, I think."

His wife appears and smiles when she sees Anne. "Thanks so much for suggesting I read A.S. Byatt. Possession was brilliant and now I'm into Angels and Insects."

"Next, The Children's Book?" Anne says, paying for her array of packages - meat and cheeses in brown waxed paper, salads in what look like new plastic containers.

"Oh yes," his wife replies. "It must be wonderful working in a library."

"Sometimes challenging, always interesting," Ann says. Just before leaving, she asks about the plastic containers.

The butcher laughs. "A new supplier," he says, obviously pleased she has noticed. "Designed to go directly from fridge to table"

"I'll be sure to let everyone know who provided my feast," she adds, hurrying out the door.

If they know about Harold, they say nothing. It's a relief, a hiatus. She always feels a little giddy after being there. She is Anne Dexter librarian and human being - no Harold, no martyrdom, no duty.

The supermarket is next and it drives her crazy as usual. She wants some decent serviettes and can only find ridiculously thin ones. By chance she finds a section carrying greeting cards and there, at the bottom of the display, a whole row of specialty serviettes. She has to choose between forget-me-nots and brilliantly coloured maple leaves. She goes for the flower pattern, ridiculously expensive, ten in a package. She dithers and takes three packages just to be sure. Next is Perrier for the abstainers and shrimp sauce. It takes much too long to find these and a few other necessitates and all the check-out lineups are a mile long.

Then to the cleaners to get Harold's precious tuxedo. She imagines they laugh behind her back - why would she want to put a quadriplegic in a tuxedo? It isn't for her to decide. Where Harold is concerned, she rarely makes decisions. She tries to remember if she did before the accident. It didn't seem to matter then. Harold was a take charge gentleman and she liked it that way. It gave her more time to read, to scribble in her spiral bound notebook, number twenty-six on its cover - twelve years' worth to date. She rarely reread anything she wrote though and thought little of it.

After she'd been at the library for a few months and confided to a colleague or two that she loved writing, several started pestering her to polish something, send it out to a magazine or publisher. What about The Globe & Mail's "Facts and Arguments" or even one of those columns in Reader's Digest? Someone else suggested a writers' group that met at the library Tuesday evenings. Reluctantly she decided to give it a try. The instructor was an inspiring vibrant soul, well published from Anne's point of view - the library had several of her books and it was evident that many of her mostly middle-aged students had been taking her course for several years.

There were some like herself who had no interest in being published and some who thought it the only worthwhile pursuit. They were given short assignments and encouraged to bring finished pieces in for group critiquing. Anne could never bring herself to do this. For starters, she would have had to enter one of her hand-written pieces into a computer and printed out copies. The thought of others reading and commenting on what she had written seemed abhorrent to her. She sat at the back of the room, wrote her in-class assignments and listened to others read what they had written. One of the members talked about getting several stories and poems published in literary magazines and, when Anne found out how many rejections this woman had endured, how many rewrites she did for each piece, she quietly bowed out of the group. This was not why she was writing. She just poured things out on the page. It made her feel lighter, mental baggage to get rid of, words to let go of and forget about. She wrote for cathartic reasons not in hope of publication.

She has dozens more journals all packed away at her parents' place. It started in grade eight with a certain teacher whose name she can't remember now wanting them to have a Daily Journal. Every morning, right after the National Anthem and Lord's Prayer, they were given twenty minutes to write. She discovered it wasn't enough time and she took hers home most evenings, writing more before bedtime. She had three journals filled by the end of the school year. Her dream pages she called them. After that she wrote on her own, bought packages of scribblers and filled them one by one. In university, side-tracked by intense essay writing, she stopped entirely but had started again with her honeymoon edition. Harold was too wrapped up in his own life to ask about her writing but then she rarely wrote anything when he was around.

Before the accident his presence absorbed her, held her captive. She basked luxuriously in the strength of his intellectual being. Now she endures occasionally fantasizing that it's all a bad dream that will go away. Often when she first wakes up on a weekend morning, she thinks for an instant that Harold is in the kitchen making coffee, that he will bring her a cup; sit on the bed and discuss some article from the morning paper.

The post office is also crowded, and she waits in line over ten minutes tapping the pick-up card impatiently against her arm. Another book on Fitzgerald Harold has ordered. Al Runston is two ahead of her.

"The elegant Anne Dexter," he says when he notices her turning in his swashbuckling manner one arm extended. "Erma and I are so looking forward to your little soireé. We always do."

Thankfully, a voice calls "next" and he swaggers to the counter turning to give her a conspiratorial wink that makes her squirm. At more than one dinner party she has separated his hand from her backside. She finds him slimy and overbearing. In an amazingly short period of time following Harold's accident, she has learned to fence with this type of man, a steel demureness she knows has gained her a reputation of self-imposed celibacy probably frigidity. She could do worse in a small town.

"The timer went off before the last commercial and that must be at least fifteen minutes ago," Harold calls as the back door slams with her first trip in. He's watching a game show.

Anne doesn't answer. She'll wait until after the party to give him the book otherwise she'll never get him dressed and ready. On her second trip in she manages to grab mail from the box. She doesn't notice the post card until she dumps everything on the kitchen table.

"There was a line up at the post office," she says, sorting through junk flyers. The post card leaps out at her. Toronto, Ontario, a picture of the CN tower.

"Did you get my tuxedo?"

She flips the card over. "Now free flying. Will be at the Bay Shore Inn, Vancouver, weekend of July 15/16. Can you be there? R.C." An address is scribbled beneath. Less than two weeks from now. She stops breathing.

"You forgot?" Harold calls. "Don't tell me you forgot."

Robert Chamberlain. She lets the breath out slowly. March library convention in Toronto. She was the only one from the library to go. She'd thrown herself into the sessions - it was wonderful to have nothing to think about but her work and herself. At the closing weekend session, after a particularly grueling evening seminar rampant with politics, she and some colleagues went down to the bar to unwind. They were already paired off - two couples - and she was sitting alone, enjoying a slow Scotch when he came over and asked if he could join her.

He was a computer consultant; lived in Toronto, his marriage on the rocks. The line was boringly familiar, and she braced herself but not quite well enough. He was polite, interesting and compellingly sensual. When he asked her to dance, she felt as though all her nerve endings were exposed. It made her giddy and definitely not herself. At the end of the set he took her for a drink and they talked for over an hour. It was so wonderful to actually communicate - she spilled out much more than she intended and then they danced again - late night dancing slow and mellow. She felt like a teenager pressed against him. When he kissed her on the dance floor, she realized she had dug her nails into his arm.

"Anne? Anne? I can't get my breath."

She rushes into the living room as Harold breaks into a spasm of violent coughing. His head rolls back and forth on the chin rest, the creases in his face accentuate. A small stream of saliva trickles down the corner of his mouth.

"It's all right," she whispers, holding his head with her hands. "I'm here, it's all right."

"You forgot my tuxedo," he chokes out finally after another spasm.

"No I didn't. It's hanging over the kitchen chair."

The coughing ceases abruptly. "What time are our guests arriving?" Perfectly normal voice.

Anne wipes his face and stands upright. "Seven," she replies wearily. "I still have to finish the laundry and get everything ready." She looks at him grey and stubborn there in the chair. He has become old and is pulling her right along with him. She will be forty the middle of September, forty going on eighty.

July fifteenth. Less than two weeks away. She returns to the counter. The card is missing. She retraces her steps into the living room.

"I thought you had things to do," Harold says. "Since you're here try a different channel for me, will you?"

She tries six channels before he is satisfied and knows her impatience shows.

"You're edgy."

"It's the party. I'm not used to getting organized for such a crowd."

"Then you'd better get at it."

She retraces her steps again, face burning. What has happened to the damn postcard?

When she inadvertently glances under the table, she sees it stuck between the two piles of dust. She snaps up the card, folds it in half and stuffs it into her jeans pocket then goes for the broom and dustpan.

After she sweeps up the strange grey substance, she can't quite bring herself to throw it away. The over-sized box Mrs. Forester used for Harold's electric bow tie is still on top of the fridge. It has a fancy lid like a chocolate box and is the perfect size. She places the box and its contents ceremoniously on the fireplace mantle in the dining room. They rarely use this *fireplace - sometimes at Christmas or if Harold wants to impress dinner guests.*

He looks up through the open French doors. He's watching a mid-day grade B movie.

"I'm cold," he says, "You should put the heat on."

"It's glorious outside," she replies, "I think we should eat lunch on the patio."

"Not today," Harold snaps firmly. "I much prefer the dining room."

There were still some sandwiches Mrs. Forester had made the day before. She really was a gem, not that she wasn't paid well for it. She treated everyone, including Harold, like a child. Anne went along with her quirky behaviour - it was easier that way.

"Peanut butter wheels and egg salad triangles," Anne reports to Harold depositing the plate on the dining room table. His eyes sparkle. She can remember being in his fourth year class when arguing Yeats or Lawrence would have done the same. She holds a peanut butter wheel to his lips. He chomps and drools a little.

"I'll get you some milk," she says. Both to the fridge and back she feels the edges of the post card in her jeans pocket.

Robert took her hand and led her to the elevator and, as they walked down the smoke-stale hallway, she realized vaguely that they must be going to his room. She didn't think she was drunk not from liquor at least and as soon as he closed the door, she felt confidently wicked.

Harold's stare jolts her back and she almost spills the glass of milk on his neck.

"Keep your mind on what you're doing," he mutters. "Off in dreamland again?"

Going to Vancouver in two weeks is out of the question. She would have to invent a reason, not only to Harold and Mrs. Forester but also to everyone at the Library. She'd have to catch the ferry over Friday afternoon and that would mean getting off work early to make a bus connection.

Of course, she could always go Saturday morning.

She gathers things up and hurries into the kitchen. A ferry schedule. Where was it? She rummages through a couple of drawers.

"Anne?" Harold calls. "It's time for my nap."

Harold has radar sensitivity whenever she's concentrating on something solely her own. It always makes her feel guilty even when perfectly innocent. This time she snaps to attention like an overly conscientious recruit.

"I'm so cold," he says as she wheels him into the bedroom. "Especially my legs."

"I'll turn on the electric blanket," she replies fluffing his pillows. "I could put the heating pad under your legs." Saying it makes her feel strangely clammy.

"Find my long underwear, will you, the heavy stuff?"

When she lifts him onto the bed, the stuffed socks and slippers fall off the foot rest, thudding gently onto the floor, a stream of grey dust sifting from each pant leg spilling into their plaid interiors.

By the time Anne arranges Harold for his nap, his eyes are closed and, even before she covers him with the crazy quilt, he's sound asleep. She sweeps up the dust and, carrying it to the dining room, deposits it into the box. She pours herself a large Scotch, puts his socks in the dryer and begins to organize the buffet.

The party is a roaring success. People keep streaming in and after eighteen Anne loses count. Everyone loves the food and she makes a point of mentioning where it was purchased. Conviviality reigns and Harold seems even brighter than usual.

"You're looking so well," Erma purrs, taking his limp hand. "Have you put on a little weight?"

Anne has her back to them and she bites the side of her glass. Given the circumstances, the long underwear was an *excellent choice on Harold's part. Anne stuffed it snugly with two old flannelette sheets. When she pulled up the neatly pressed tuxedo pants, he looked almost muscular.*

Now she thinks she may have overdone it.

"It must be Mrs. Forester's good cooking," Anne breaks in, simultaneously making a hundred and eighty degree turn and snatching a woolly throw from the back of the couch. She engineers herself between Erma and the front of the wheelchair. "Harold's been so cold lately, haven't you dear," she purrs. "Here, I'll tuck this around you."

"I'm not cold right now," Harold hisses in her ear.

"There we are," she continues. "That's better." It does make him look slightly less sturdy.

It's past two AM before all the guests leave. Harold is somewhat drunk and very pliable. He even smiles at her when she tucks the quilt under his chin.

She cleans up everything before even thinking about bed. Harold will make such a fuss the following morning if she doesn't. Besides, it gives her the opportunity to have another Scotch. She fuzzily supposes it isn't good to be drinking alone - giggles at her decadence - pours another. She only does this after dinner parties. Iron clad rule. She knows too well what happens to women in difficult situations, drinking some and then more to cope: her grandmother, who nursed a husband incapacitated by a stroke, an aunt whose brother had some mysteriously degenerating disease. She tries not to think about them - one generation after the other, duty in the name of love.

After she empties the last ashtray and puts her glass in the sink, she tiptoes into her bedroom. No more maudlin thoughts. She undresses in the dark, a well-worn habit. Harold never showed any interest in looking at her naked body. It never occurred to her anyone would.

She retrieves the postcard from her jeans pocket; sets it upright against her lamp and lies down in the cooling darkness.

That unexpected spring liaison was like a dream now - an incredible dream forgotten until this damn postcard arrived.

She can barely remember either of them undressing - the whole thing was so urgent, so uninhibited. He turned on music and they danced together naked. She remembered that skin on skin with the lights on.

Their mutual lust drove them onto one other with a fury she had never before experienced. A novel experience participating - enthusiasm and sexual creativity she had only read about in fiction. All the clichés washed over her - she loved every minute of it.

The phone rings.

Anne bolts upright to answer. If Harold wakes, he will take hours to calm down.

"Hello..."

"Yes, I'm fine. Why?"

"What? Oh god..." She slams the receiver, pressing one hand over the other to stop both from shaking. Al Runston, even though he didn't say so. Harold's poor neglected wife...and he magnanimously wanted to help. The worst part is she'd have to be civil to him at the next party. What an arrogant bastard he was. Is she that obviously horny? She doesn't think so. Certainly not when he's around her. Can't he tell she loathes him? She could see this going on for years. They would all get old and musty, having their ridiculous little parties year after year and Al all wizened up and probably sexually useless would still be pinching her bottom and making late night semi-obscene phone calls.

Anne slips back to the kitchen; pours another Scotch; drinks it like a shooter, then falls into bed and is out.

IV

Sunday morning when Harold finally calls for her it's after nine and she has a raging headache. She's almost afraid to go into his room and, when she reaches around behind his back and feels his ribs, she sighs audibly.

"You've got bad breath," he chides.

"Sorry." .It doesn't even upset her.

On Sundays there is a ritual to follow. Half grapefruit followed by waffles - always a messy and tedious business. Anne puts the postcard in the kitchen drawer so she can fantasize strategies.

The morning after had been equally wonderful. She didn't hate herself and he wasn't distant, quite the opposite. They had a leisurely breakfast in the dining room and later, after a prolonged and rather obvious parting, she sat in her room, considering how to deal with the enormity of the past few hours in relation to her real life. Thankfully she slept on the plane back to Vancouver, crying only on the ferry facing into the wind, letting cold spray clear her face and memory. She would return to duty and her former life.

"The grapefruit needs more sugar." Harold complains and then, "Why isn't there real maple syrup?"

Anne sighs. "They didn't have any at the supermarket."

"What about that specialty place?"

"They get it from Ontario. When I checked last week, they said not for another ten days."

"You didn't check yesterday?"

"I didn't have time, really. I..."

Harold spits the mouthful of waffle back onto his plate. "It's lumpy," he says. "Peel me an orange."

Anne stands at the kitchen sink, pulling the peel from the orange with a spoon. A small corner of Cassandra Bay glimmers through a break in the distant trees. What she needs to do is go for a swim. Through the winter months mornings before work, she goes to the area Rec Centre, swimming forty to sixty lengths front crawl, her mind numbing aware only of her arms gliding through the water, up for air down and forward. Once it's warm enough, usually sometime in July at lunch times, she swims in the Bay. The changing rooms aren't crowded as most people don't swim. It is always brutally cold at first but she toughens up.

That first crack into sea water icicle cold pulling the breath out of her, front crawl at top speed until she feels numb, then a steady stroke for ten fifteen maybe twenty minutes before she turns and heads back. If she gets there a little before noon and is lucky, there are no boats in the bay and, she swims straight out stroke following stroke, the splash and catch of her own breath drawing her forward until she fuses with the water, a fluid line rolling with the waves reaching out toward the horizon. Sometimes on the way out, she fantasizes of not making that one hundred and eighty degree turn back to shore of continuing straight out, disappearing. She sighs. No salt water swimming yet this year.

"Are you growing that orange out there?" Harold calls.

When she returns with the orange sections, she thinks his sleeves lie a little too closely against the body of his shirt. She keeps a blanket permanently tucked from his shoulders to his feet now. His face has a pallid grey tinge, and his eyes follow her every move.

"We're going out this morning," he announces, "right after breakfast."

They always go out on Sundays and he always reminds her. She nods, waiting until he swallows before putting another orange section to his lips. Sometimes he clamps his mouth shut and closes his eyes. She must hold the section close to his lips, often until her arm aches. The instant she moves away however, he opens his mouth and if she doesn't respond instantly, he goes into a tirade. Once in a moment of weakness, she shoved something in prematurely. He coughed and sputtered and spit it back accusing her of trying to choke him to death.

"Are you leaving that mess on the kitchen table?" he asks as she wheels him toward the front room. If she cleans up first, he berates her for being slow and if she attempts to move him first, he complains she is messy.

The front room is rarely used now except for parties. Anne watches Harold scrutinize it for something she hasn't cleaned up. It seems odd that he will notice an ashtray or an empty glass, but he hasn't observed that gradually over the past year, she has removed a number of their more favourite artifacts. Two water colours, the small nude sculpture they bought long ago at a local artisan show, an antique side table given them by his parents. Maybe these were things she only thought he cared about.

She wheels him on through, stops by the hall closet and opens it to get his jacket.

"My fingernails need cutting," he announces.

"Now?"

"Of course, now." He glowers at her.

She looks at his sleeves, plaid on plaid, with only the fold at the edge denoting the sleeve's presence against the body of the shirt. She is sure his arms are gone. The flat cuffs disappear beneath the blanket. She shudders involuntarily.

"I'll get the nail scissors," she says, heading for the bathroom. His back is to her and she makes an abrupt turn, quietly back-tracking to the basement stairway. She will have to be creative. Gardening gloves. She's sure there is a new pair she hasn't used yet.

"Why are you going down to the basement?" His hearing is still impeccable.

"The... the oil can," she calls back. "I think your wheelchair has a squeak."

"My nails," he snaps irritably. "The wheelchair's fine."

The gloves are lodged on a shelf up high in the stairwell. She has to reach up to retrieve them and when she does, one falls out of sight through an open step.

"The sump pump's making a funny noise," she calls, racing down to retrieve it. "I'd better check." She has always been adept at verbal side-stepping. A snappy answer usually slows his rapid-fire attack.

Moments later in the kitchen, she stuffs the gloves with Kleenex, returning to the back door closet for his wind breaker.

"I don't know what's taking you so long," he says, "surely, you've checked everything by now."

"Oh my," she says with forced surprise, "the zipper on your wind breaker seems to be stuck."

"It wasn't when we took it off last."

"I borrowed it when I went out to pick roses."

"You borrowed my wind breaker?"

"I couldn't find mine and it was spitting rain."

He gave her his oh-my-god-you're-inferior look. "It helps if you keep things in their proper place."

She stands at the kitchen counter, carefully pinning the bulging gloves to the wind breaker. Three tea towels for each sleeve. A soft sculpture doll, she thinks, a modern-day Raggedy Andy

When she pulls Harold forward to position the back of the jacket, he's half-asleep his eyes closed. When it's zipped up, she tucks the bulging gloves in under the blanket. Most of the dust is still in the wheelchair. This time, she ignores it.

He snores a couple of times and then, with a snort opens his eyes to stare at her. "My nails?" he says again, as if she were a negligent six year-old.

"It's getting late," she says, "couldn't we please wait until after?" She's the child now, begging. She is probably also crazy or going crazy.

Harold closes his eyes and hums.

Anne puts on her jacket and hopes he'll forget about his damned nails. Or lack of them.

"Get the coin then," he snaps, finally.

They use an old silver dollar taken from Harold's precious collection; the coin given to him by an American uncle when Harold was a boy. Anne takes the coin from its small padded box in the hall table drawer and places it conspicuously on the dark wood surface. On to the next, she thinks. Thank God for small mercies.

As she wheels Harold alongside the table, he looks up and smiles. She wishes she could remember what his smile used to be like. After the accident, he made her put all photographs of him away. She must have them hidden somewhere and can't remember. His face is skeletal now, almost an apparition.

She ceremoniously flips the coin. It twirls on the table's shiny surface and lands.

"Heads I win," he says with childish glee, "tails you lose."

Anne doesn't bother to get upset about this anymore.

"I win again," he repeats gleefully. He pauses as though contemplating alternatives. The answer has been basically the same as on all warm weather days throughout the last year. "We'll go out in the canoe," he says.

During the cold rainy months, he always chose a ride in the van. Once or twice Anne suggested a change - a picnic or a movie. He would either hum or choke according to her degree of insistence. It was easier to give in.

The venerable Chevy van, adapted to accommodate the wheelchair in place of the passenger seat, is equipped with a platform that moves out and down onto the end of the cedar plank sidewalk leading from the house ramp. Anne always marvels at this, remembering how the carpenter insisted she position the van ramp in down position so he could measure and build the walk accordingly.

It's only a twenty-minute drive down to the dock and old Herb Stinson always helps her get Harold into the canoe. She worries a little about the dust in the wheelchair but Herb doesn't seem to notice. He's too busy making sure the canoe is lodged tightly against the dock before he helps Anne shift Harold down into it.

"Is it the red canoe?" Harold asks almost accusingly as if it might not be.

"Of course it's the red canoe," Anne says, grinning at Herb who gives her a wink.

He makes no comment about how light Harold has become but then he wouldn't. Above all things, old Herb is polite. The last couple of Sundays, Harold has only wanted to stay out on the water a short time and she wonders it if will be worth it today.

The day is glorious. As she paddles along the rocky shore line, gulls fly out from the craggy rocks and the sun streams through the overhanging trees. Her euphoria is short-lived.

"My feet are cold," Harold announces, barely five minutes after they've set out. She puts the paddle up and leans precariously forward to adjust the blanket. Next it's his hands then his knees. Anne finds it increasingly more difficult to paddle. Her head screams the insanity of it all: the ridiculousness of these requests, the irrationality of words, thought of existence itself, back and forth until she has stomach cramps.

When she mistakenly turns them in toward shore for the third time in as many minutes, Harold quips, "What's the matter, losing your touch?"

"Maybe we should go back," she says. "I seem to be a little tired."

"Your problem is you drank too much last night."

"I did not."

"I do still have the power of observation," he replies.

Anne concentrates on the paddle, the water, the shore.

V

After supper that evening, Anne settles Harold in front of the TV and makes a bee line to his bedroom. For propriety's sake, she feels she must prepare a pajama top suitably. She dithers about the gloves and makes a mental note to go to the hardware store on the way home Monday and pick up some more gardening gloves. After a bit of searching, she finds in the bottom of one of his drawers, a soft leather pair wrapped in tissue paper inside an elegant box, a small card in an envelope on top. She can't resist opening it. "To dear Robbie for your wild rides." Love and kisses Auntie Jan. Now here's a part of Harold's life she knows nothing about. Probably a former sports car. He did like to drive fast. She sighs and stuffs the gloves and, pinning each one to his pajama top sleeve, stops to admire her handwork. With the pajama top sleeves already plumped out with underwear, the effect is quite respectable. She hangs it up in the closet for later and imagines his clothes cupboard filled with padded shirts, each with their own set of gloves. Aspects of Harold's torso she thinks ruefully - if only she could change his head.

She sits on the bed for a few minutes attempting to rally her strength and suddenly remembers from childhood, one of the Oz book stories: the queen who had a cabinet full of heads, all equally grand and decorated, each bearing a different mood. In the morning she would rise and consider which head to use. Will I be haughty today or frivolous, patient or overbearing? Her head would determine how she interacted with her courtiers, what decisions she made concerning her people. Even as a child Anne remembers thinking how wonderful that would be, that there would be no guilt or remorse over decisions or actions, one would simply put on a different head that had no memory of previous words or activities. One of author Frank L. Baum's marvelous commentaries on the human race and it applied here to Harold.

It was as if he had switched heads. Not remotely a rational conclusion but comforting under the circumstances.

"What have you been up to?" Harold says, looking up when she finally appears from the bedroom.

"Clean sheets on your bed," she replies, pleased with her fast come back.

"Not those scratchy new ones I hope."

"No Harold. I'm giving those an extra wash."

Harold grunts and turns back to the TV. Anne sits off to one side trying to read a novel she brought from the library. It's not that well written and the author's flippant style annoys her. Maybe it's just that everything annoys her. She looks over at Harold her knight in shining armour, most of it now rusted and fallen off. She should be sympathetic, caring. She was at the beginning but now, now she has become as bitter as he is.

That night after she arranges Harold in bed, Anne takes the post card out to the kitchen table, reads it once more then tries to compose an answer. She knows she'll have to rewrite it several times, that whatever it is that she wants to say will have to be pulled from her brain, dragged past the guilt and duty holding the words back. She tiptoes to her bedroom to retrieve her latest spiral notebook thinking that if she pretends she's just writing, she can trick her brain and come up with something clever. She enters the date as she always does and then sits writing short pithy sentences and crossing them out again.

Once she has a composed a decent sentence, she'll copy it onto something suitable for mailing. "Would love to see you but in work overload." Crossed out. "Would love to see you but can't leave Harold right now." Crossed out. "Would love to see you again if I can get things organized to get away." She adds "Dear RC" at the beginning and "AD" at the end. She stares at the two letters for a moment. AD. Anne Dexter but also Anno Domini, Before Christ, the calendar system used with the Julian and Gregorian calendars, the term from Medieval Latin.

It suits her present condition, something no longer functional, abandoned by scholars if she remembers correctly. A tear falls onto the paper then another soaking rapidly into a large wet spot. Without thinking, she rubs it with her fist only to smudge the letters and tear the paper. Her conscience tells her this was for a reason, that she should rip the page out and throw the paper away; abandon this mad plan. She smooths the torn place and shuffles thorough a pile of envelopes and flyers, willfully silencing her own thoughts.

One of those notepads from worthy organizations surfaces. This one says A note from... Anne Dexter at the top, lines to write on and an exquisite Monarch butterfly poised on an Echinacea flower at the bottom. She snatches it up and positions her scant message in the middle, toys with signing her full name but leaves it with AD, folds and slips the paper into an envelope pulled from one of Harold's desk organizers. She knows he must despair at the chaos everywhere especially on tables and desks. "A place for everything and everything in its place," he always says. Magazines in one pile, flyers in another, letters sorted as to priority. She sighs and copies Rob's name and address on the envelope. As she licks it shut, guilt squeezes her throat and stomach rendering her queasy. What happened the first time was spontaneous. This is deliberate and premeditated. Almost like murder.

As she writes his Toronto, Ontario address on the envelope, it occurs to her he must have gone to some lengths to get her address, unless of course, he looked in her purse when she was still asleep. She slept soundly enough and he was already up when she woke. Every time she replays it, the scene becomes more dream-like.

When she opened her eyes and realized she wasn't in her own room, she was momentarily terrified. She looked up and he was grinning at her, pants partly done up, chest bare. She was acutely aware of her own nakedness and felt her nipples harden under the sheet. He pulled the sheet back and began nibbling in a circle around her navel. She grabbed his shoulders, making noises she had no idea she could make, and they made love in broad daylight. Afterward he excused himself discreetly to the bathroom. She dressed hurriedly and they walked sedately down for breakfast. She remembers feeling so debauched, being sure it must show.

She stares at the envelope. The few lines she has written are friendly but purposely vague. Better to keep her options open, especially under the circumstances.

VI

Before Mrs. Forester arrives on Monday morning Anne panics. After Harold was asleep last night, she removed the gardening gloves from his wind breaker and pinned them to a plumped up shirt on the chair at the end of his bed. More than a dozen times, she has rehearsed what she will say to her about Harold's new circumstances but, whenever she thinks about it, she develops stress pains in her chest and has to sit down.

He calls for her even before she manages a sip from her first cup of coffee. When she looks in the bedroom door, her head spins a little and she leans heavily against the dresser.

"You're not getting sick, are you?" Harold says. "There's only room for one of us in that category." It's the closest he has come to saying he needs her.

"No, I'm fine," Anne replies, opening his curtains. "You're awake early this morning."

"Busy day ahead," he says gruffly. "Is Mrs. Forester late?"

"No Harold, it's not eight o'clock yet."

"She's supposed to be here at seven thirty."

"It's always been eight."

"Well, tell her seven thirty from now on."

She fleetingly thinks of suggesting she will dress him for the day but, knowing it will initiate a tirade refrains and instead, asks him if he wants the bedroom TV on. When he grunts to the affirmative, she finds a morning talk show and quietly leaves.

After pouring a fresh cup of coffee, she sits in the kitchen, staring out at a blue speck of the Bay. This morning it looks like a misplaced puzzle piece, art deco on a surreal landscape. She feels like two people - one on the brink of unpardonable escape, one duty bound and grounded.

"You're not even dressed girl, are you sick?" Mrs. Forester appears in the back doorway, apron slung over her arm.

Anne leaps up. "Slept in," she manages to say, racing for her bedroom. You mustn't be late, she thinks. Unheard of.

Anne Dexter is never late for work. At work she is organized and punctual. It's only here she slacks off. Whatever was she thinking? Daydreaming, procrastinating. Avoiding reality.

Ten minutes later when she disappears out the door, Mrs. Forester is already cooing over Harold. What there is left of him, Anne thinks to herself. Well Mrs. Forester will have to deal with it. Who knows, maybe she won't notice. As the door clicks shut, her library life clicks in - a report to finish, two meetings and a replacement summer student in for an interview. She sheds Harold, Mrs. Forester, her domestic responsibility; slithers out of it like a snake shedding its skin.

The day is full of unexpected deadlines and continual hassles. The CEO has called in sick and Anne has to assume some of her responsibilities. Someone throws up in the women's washroom, two books are missing from the Recent Releases display and a part-time staffer appears in her doorway in tears saying she can't find the keys to one of the storage closets. Anne barely has time for lunch. She realizes on the way home, she hasn't mailed the letter. "Tomorrow," she says aloud as she's driving. "It will still have time to get there if I mail it tomorrow."

Anne does remember to go to the hardware store for gloves. There's a special on - six pairs of cotton gardening gloves for $5.99. The woman at the checkout beams. "Another gardener," she gushes, ringing in the sale. "I always know who's into planting and pruning, such a wonderful hobby." She hands Anne her gloves in a small plastic bag. Anne nods and gives her a forced smile. More like grafting than pruning, she thinks ruefully as she gets back in her car.

She drives home slowly and stays in the van a few minutes before going into the house. It looks exactly the same as it always has - dark green shutters she was so taken with the first time she saw it, an expansive cedar deck on the west side, protected by huge evergreens, slices of the Bay in view when there is a breeze. The same yet irrevocably different, a haven turned prison. "Don't be melodramatic," she says to herself. "Keep things in perspective."

Mrs. Forester is bustling about preparing supper. "Harold's been so good today, haven't you Harold?" A bowl of partly eaten orange sherbet is on the table, a little trickling down Harold's chin.

His face tightens visibly when Anne appears.

"And how is the great world of library science today?"

Standard question.

"As usual."

Standard answer, safe and non-threatening to both parties.

"I must be off," Mrs. Forester chirps. She dabs a fluffy pink face cloth around the corners of Harold's mouth. "We've dictated another fascinating episode of Professor Dexter's life into the tape recorder," she says. "Such a brilliant man you have in your life."

Anne nods, attempting to smile.

"Cheerio," Mrs. Forester adds, throwing Harold a kiss. "See you tomorrow."

Anne watches Harold, the longing in his face. Parting is such sweet sorrow, she thinks. The thought occurs to her that he may be in love with the woman.

"Such a wonderful human being," Harold says, "so selfless, so cheerful."

"A gem," Anne replies. It's one of her standard comments regarding Mrs. Forester, certainly true and suitably vague. She sorts through the mail she's just retrieved.

Another postcard. Toronto by Night - silhouette of a couple on a balcony. She flips it over. Arriving a week early. How about Sunday at six in the Bay Shore Inn lounge? R.C. His smile appears and hovers in front of her like the Cheshire cat's. Sunday, he was asking her to be there this Sunday? She'd have to see if Mrs. Forester could work on Sunday and stay overnight, as well as make arrangements to take Monday off.

Find someone to cover for her. She trembles. What if they read postcards down at the post office?

"What's for supper?"

Anne sticks the post card under a flyer and goes to the stove. "Looks like Beef Bourguignonne," she says. "When do you want to eat?"

"Now."

"Right now?"

"Are you deaf?"

"But you just had ice cream." She knows she's stalling, wanting a few minutes to think. Her preoccupation is impetus for attack.

"It was sherbet."

"What I meant was..."

"I don't care what you meant. I want my supper: candles, linen, my tweed jacket, red wine with the beef. We must maintain decorum; continue life as it always has been."

Anne wants to scream at him that it isn't the same, not even remotely the same, that it has veered from previous reality almost to a point of no return. Wants to but doesn't. She is an adult and has learned to harness her anger, channel it. She presses it out through her fingertips as she sets the table with cloth and candles. As she maneuvers Harold into a white stuffed shirt and his tweed jacket, the lightness of his torso is a renewed shock. The shoulders are ridiculously large and, as she tucks the new garden gloves in under the blanket, she realizes Mrs. Forester hasn't said anything.

"How did Mrs. Forester make out today?" she asks as she pours wine into two crystal glasses.

"Are you jealous of her?" he asks, grinning one of his infrequent grins.

"Of Mrs. Forester?"

The accusation comes as a shock.

"Perhaps you should be," he adds.

The conversation is again in his court, a manoeuver into unknown territory, a fencing match in the arena of the absurd.

"I'm delighted with Mrs. Forester," she says effusively as she sips some wine into Harold's mouth. "I'm delighted that you're delighted."

"Boringly repetitive," he says, "Why don't you try the thesaurus?"

"Repetition for emphasis."

Anne inhales her first glass of wine and pours another.

Later, after watching the news on TV, Anne notices that Harold's head lies rather heavily against the chin rest.

"My neck and shoulders ache," he complains. "I think you'd better give me a back rub."

As she wheels him into the bedroom, his padded arms slowly sink in toward each other until they dangle under his head. Anne takes a deep breath. Getting him into bed is going to be a challenge. What she needs is a distraction. She slips a Mozart flute concerto into the portable CD player and turns the volume up, a bedtime ritual from before the accident. Harold closes his eyes and hums off key.

Music to soothe the savage beast.

She tiptoes to the dresser and pulls out a handful of his pajama bottoms to use as stuffing. Some dust has already trickled out the front of his shirt and accumulated in a tidy pile in the crotch of his pants. What I should do she thinks, is pick him up and shake him like a mop.

Her potential giggle dissolves in the macabre business of stuffing enough pajama bottoms into the shirt he's wearing. When she buttons him up again, he groans a little and asks her again to rub his neck. She adjusts his collar and, concentrating on breathing at an even pace, cautiously works up the neck muscles to his hair line and back down. The second time she does this, his face relaxes visibly. She slowly pulls the crazy quilt up around his chin and he's asleep before she turns off the light.

Between Scotches, Anne flips through a couple of books and five or six magazines before turning on the TV. She changes channels at least a dozen times and, after the third too large shot of Scotch, starts undressing the good-looking men on the TV screen - the broad-shouldered ones with good asses. After a while, they all look like Rob. If there is any possibility of escape, any conjuring up of a desperate scenario, she will grab it, play out her lustful romance heroine scene, escape into a turbulent landscape of her own fabrication. Consequences be damned. She pours herself another Scotch and falls asleep on the couch.

For the next three days, she is so distracted by work, she forgets entirely about mailing the envelope. First thing Thursday morning, sitting at her desk, she's rummaging through her purse for her check book - one of the summer students is running in a charity race and wants a pledge - and the letter surfaces. She tells the front desk she has to pick up a prescription and runs all the way to the post office - Priority Post $12.42, guaranteed to arrive the next day - the post office person assures her.

When she looks at the pile on her desk, she knows she will have to work right through lunch to be ready for the afternoon Board meeting. They're a particular bunch, most of them retired conscientious do-gooders and she must be on her toes. Anne can smell her own sweat as soon as she sits down in the Boardroom. She still finds these sessions awkward. They're always fresh and ready for action, assuming she will have all the answers, solve all the problems. Then the usual petty political wrangling ensues making it impossible to concentrate and she is so preoccupied, she says the same thing three times in a row. They know she's under stress and is thankful that no one trips her up for it.

There's a note on her desk when she arrives back just before five. "Maple syrup is in." She smiles and dashes for her car, hoping to make it to the shop before their five thirty closing.

VII

Friday morning Mrs. Forester arrives fifteen minutes early, looking more than a little rattled. She glances toward the bedroom and, when she hears Harold still snoring, beckons Anne to come closer.

"I'm so sorry to tell you this on such short notice, dear," she begins quietly. "My brother-in-law called yesterday at supper time to say my only sister has had a stroke and is in hospital on the mainland."

"How awful," Anne says. "You must go and see her right away."

"I thought if you could come home a bit early, I could catch the late afternoon ferry and be there by this evening."

"Of course, by all means."

The day disappears like a phantom and Anne tries to remember what she was to do Friday afternoon. Loose ends Friday they call it, the day to finalize things not done, yet to do. "I could be home by two thirty, I think."

Mrs. Forester nods and rests her hand on Anne's arm. "I know this will upset our Harold, so I think it best to say nothing for now."

Anne nods.

"Should it become necessary for me to stay longer..." She pauses and looks out the window. "I've taken the liberty of asking two of my friends - either would be willing - to fill in for a few days if necessary." She tucks a piece of paper into Anne's hand, straightens her shoulders and disappears into Harold's room. Anne hears her say in her usual jaunty voice, "Well now, how is my sleepy-head Harold? Not roused himself yet?" She hears some giggling and then Mrs. Forester reappears.

"I wanted to ask you," Anne says, taking the van keys from their hook, "how has Harold been this last week?"

"Why fine," Mrs. Forester says cheerfully, taking breakfast things from the cupboard. "A bit frailer perhaps, but surprisingly cheerful given the circumstances."

Anne weighs the words for inference. It's impossible to tell whether or not there is any. She wonders who is playing this charade and who is just pretending to play.

She tucks the piece of paper in her purse and makes a mental note to contact both these women to see if either would be available Sunday.

On the way to work, she thinks about the illusion of existence from one of her Philosophy classes, the scenario lighting up as if yesterday. Some guy in the front row, mat of curly blonde hair, arguing vociferously that the external world outside one's own mind was unsure and therefore might not exist; two or three others around her railing to the contrary. The professor loved this interchange and egged them all on – for two or three classes. Anne read and listened but in the end was unsure. Ostensibly, the argument was ridiculous even though the front row guy made it seem feasible. She wonders now, thinking of Harold from his point of view, does anything exist outside his mind? Paradoxically, could this include his own body? The library sign looms and she switches into work mode.

That morning, after five phone calls to co-workers, she gives up in disgust. No one is available Monday. She's left it too late - the exit sign flickers.

When she returns home just after two-thirty, Harold and Mrs. Forester are laughing over something she's been reading to him.

"You didn't tell me Mrs. Forester was leaving early," he says accusingly.

"Now Harold," Mrs. Forester replies, patting his shoulder, "I only told your dear wife this morning just before she left for work."

"If you'd come in to say goodbye," he went on, "you could have told me."

Anne refrains from saying that there wasn't really time, that Mrs. Forester had told her just as she was going out the door, that he's always grumpy when he first wakes up and doesn't want her prattling away at him - his very words every time she does try to say goodbye.

"Well I must be off," Mrs. Forester says, thankfully interrupting this ad nauseam train of thought. "I'll call you Sunday evening."

"You'll be here Monday?" Harold cuts in, his eyes darting back and forth from one to the other, almost as if he knows.

"I certainly plan to," Mrs. Forester replies cheerfully. "I'm making a short trip to the mainland to visit family and plan to be back on the late Sunday afternoon ferry." She nods to Anne and hurries out the door.

VIII

When Harold goes into a coughing fit on Saturday morning after breakfast, Anne fleetingly enacts the hospital scenario as a solution.

"Do something," he keeps sputtering between spasms. "For god's sakes, do something." She gives him several sips of water; considers whacking him on the back but is afraid he will end up on the floor.

"Since you can't seem to do anything useful, put me back to bed. If I'm going to die, I want to be lying down for it."

"You're not going to die," Anne says, pushing the wheelchair back to the bedroom.

"We're all going to die," Harold says in his most acerbic tone of voice. "Or do you have access to some preferential information of which I'm not aware."

"What I meant..."

"The trouble with you is that you've never learned to think before you speak."

"I'm sorry, I didn't..."

Harold coughs again, a forced cough this time, a signal that the conversation is over. If Anne persists, he will hum. She arranges him in the bed, pulls up the coverlet and marches out.

And if she did rush him to the hospital, how would she explain his situation to the nurses, a doctor? She still thinks fleetingly that she's imagining it all; that she's moved into some altered reality, some bizarre twist in her neuron receptors that make her adjust what is to this strange version of what might be. She remembers her fascination with the neurologist turned author, Oliver Sacks, who wrote about the man who mistook his wife for a hat. He suffered from a condition called visual agnosia, the inability of the brain to translate what was actually there, to replace it with whatever he remembered seeing, in this case his hat. Anne doesn't have any floppy dolls in her bedroom, no stuffed animals either. There are some at the library in the Children's Centre but she rarely goes there. Apparently, the condition is caused by a blow to the back of the head. This doesn't apply to her either unless she has forgotten some incident, certainly not anything recent. Harold sustained head injuries even with the air bags, so if anyone saw reality altered it should be him.

Perhaps this explains it. He sees himself falling apart, disappearing and somehow, these thoughts are being transferred to his reality. It's all too bizarre and far-fetched and just adds to her stress. It does give her a superficial answer, however. The woman who mistook her husband for a soft sculpture doll. She hasn't checked the box on the mantle recently. It may be empty. That would be reassuring but, even if she is imagining it and was able to get Harold into the hospital for the weekend, he would still expect her to visit afternoon and evening. If she didn't, he would make a terrible fuss and the nurses would phone. Not a feasible option.

To make things more morose it begins raining, a pelting relentless rain that blurs the outside landscape. Harold wakens in a foul mood demanding hot chocolate and marshmallows.

When it rains, we always have hot chocolate," he says too many times while she is preparing it. "And we sit in front of the fire."

There is no wood by the fireplace and by the time Anne finds her yellow slicker, trudges to the back shed and back for more, Harold is into a tirade. "I don't know what takes you so long. The chocolate is likely cold by now or burnt."

She did have the foresight to turn off the burner before getting the fire ready and as soon as she lights the match, she hightails it back to the stove to reheat the chocolate.

The fire is a success, the drink more of a frustration. Harold coughs the marshmallows onto the tile floor in front of the fireplace and dribbles most of the hot chocolate onto his shirt.

"Read to me," he says, after she cleans up the floor and sponges his shirt. "Poetry."

Anne scans the adjacent bookshelf. "Yeats? she says, getting up to find a suitable volume. "Or Browning?"

"The poetry Mrs. Forester was reading. Over there." His eyes move from one side to the other, as if scanning the room.

Anne searches on the dining room table, several side tables, the kitchen table, nothing. "Maybe she took it with her."

"Of course she didn't," Harold says. "She found the book here. Your name was in the front of it. Anne Harrison. Miss know it all."

"From high school? University?"

"How the hell would I know?"

Anne searches the room again. Harold never swore before the accident. He picked it up from watching TV. Tough detectives, hard done by husbands.

Poetry for High School Students. On the floor by the window bench. "Here it is," she says remembering now Mrs. Forester and Harold giggling over by the window, his wheelchair facing out to the lawn and evergreens.

"The Cremation of Sam McGee," he says gleefully. "Read that one."

Her high school text - wherever did Mrs. Forester find this? Grade ten. Nasal-voiced Mr. Bebee droning out poem after poem, making them memorize one and recite it to the class.

"What about "The Highwayman?" she suggests impulsively. The one she memorized, the dashing highwayman, the dark-haired maiden bound with her fingers on the musket trigger, waiting to hear the horse's hoof beats, killing herself to save her lover. The road was a ribbon of moonlight...

"Sam McGee."

After the third time through The Arctic trails have their secret tales, that would make your blood run cold, Anne insists it's lunch time. Harold is quiet during lunch, seemingly calmed by the florid verse. Not that she minds these old gems, more that she's shocked by Harold's new preference, he a PhD

English graduate, his thesis on the legacy of Ireland's poets. She has a copy in her office; has reread it several times.

She falls asleep on the couch after arranging Harold for his afternoon nap. Wakens to him calling, coughing again, choking, spittle everywhere. For supper, he insists on Mrs. Forester's mushroom soup. A good half of it ends up on Harold and the floor. By bedtime Anne is exhausted. He's so light now, her straw man and she resists the urge to toss him into bed. When she arranges him more respectably, he stares hard at her as if he knows.

"Sing me a lullaby," he says, his voice barely audible.

She sang one when he was first in hospital, holding his then two strong hands in hers, pressing on their lifelessness, trying to force the impossible.

Given today's events, she isn't sure she can manage it. She thinks about Sam McGee, his body rendered dust; stares out the window. The night sky is a dark hollow.

"You can't remember it, I suppose," he quips.

She sits down beside him and hums the first line...

IX

The moon wakes her at four and she sleeps very little after that. The solution comes full blown like a series of power point frames. She checks them several times to make sure nothing is left out. Uncertainty and possible failure still lie in dark spaces between three of the frames. Luck and nerve will have to bridge these, making the potential precariousness temper her will, daring her to make the plan work.

Just before sunrise, she slips out of bed and tiptoes into the kitchen. Harold's snores echo gently from the other room. She makes coffee and writes out a detailed list of what must be done. By the time Harold calls her several hours later, she has over half the items checked off the list, her nap sack packed, hair in a long braid, breakfast organized, waffles cooked and in the warming oven.

"You've been up for a while," he observes when she comes into his bedroom.

"It's a glorious day," she says, opening the double windows. When she leans out, the sweetness of morning air renders her giddy.

The charade is under way. She must keep a tight rein on herself. "Would you like breakfast on the patio?" she asks.

"Is there a breeze?" he counters petulantly, "You know I can't tolerate a breeze."

She closes the windows part way. "It's delightfully warm," she replies, "and the waffles are ready."

As she wheels him toward the patio, Anne feels light-headed, confident. This will be her best performance.

"Remember when we used to take a bottle of wine out in the canoe?" she calls. She's in the kitchen putting the waffles onto two plates. Harold doesn't answer. "I thought it might be fun to take one today."

"I haven't decided that's what I want to do today," he says petulantly.

Anne freezes, her hand in mid-air. She's blown it, made the usual assumption which would normally be the case but with the fatal mistake of initiating before he has voiced his request. Somehow, she has to back track; make this work. Say something to give him the upper hand. "Silly me", she calls. "Of course you haven't. Whatever you want to do is what I want to do."

"We have to flip the coin before I decide."

"Lots of time," she says, bringing his waffles and setting them in front of him. "And see," she adds, placing the bottle ceremoniously on the table, "real maple syrup."

"Maple syrup," he says, smiling an almost genuine smile. "You didn't forget."

"Of course, I didn't." She pours an ample amount onto his waffles. Thanks to an early delivery at the Specialty Store she knows she has tipped the scale back in her favour; that the day will now progress as planned.

After Harold's somewhat messy and unsuccessful waffle consumption, he surprises Anne by saying he wants to stay on the deck a while.

"It is glorious out here," she says. "I'll just clean up before we flip the coin."

She puts the dishes in the sink out of Harold's sight line and returns to the picnic basket, slipping the wine bottle inside and Xing it off the list. In spite of her renewed assurance that her plan is underway, her pencil keeps shaking so that the X's are all wobbly. She locates an old pair of light running shoes, makes a mental note to wear a thin belt and lastly, finds a large beach towel. She takes the one with dolphins on it and, fitting it in over the wine bottle, closes the lid. Impulsively she crumples the list, then straightens it, tearing the paper into small pieces. There must be no evidence.

"The boat," he says, after the usual coin toss. "We'll go on the boat."

Later, as the platform slowly elevates him into the van, Harold asks, "Why are you wearing a skirt?" Normally she would be flattered, taking this as an indication he still notices her, perhaps even appreciatively, but today it only heightens her apprehension.

"I don't know," she says, faking carelessness, "Something different I guess." Her hand shakes as she opens the driver's door. As soon as the engine starts, Harold closes his eyes. Lately the slightest motion lulls him to into a doze. Anne is grateful for the short respite. The engine's drone fills the space between Harold's counterfeit calm and her adrenaline-charged tenseness.

"You're here bright and early this morning," Herb comments when she parks the van in its usual spot close to the dock. She's not sure what to do with the keys and finally decides to put them in the glove compartment and leave the van unlocked. One last humanitarian gesture.

"Such a perfect day," Anne hears herself say, hoping she doesn't sound unnatural. Herb doesn't seem to notice or, at least he doesn't show it. He retrieves Harold's favourite red canoe from the boat house, and she watches it splash into the water. A voice in her head says - you are insane to attempt this, think of the ramifications later. She quells it as she concentrates on Herb carefully maneuvering the canoe up close to the dock, waiting as always with a smile.

Anne positions the picnic basket strategically in the middle under the centre strut and helps Herb lower Harold down onto the end seat. Harold rarely speaks during this exercise. She knows he finds it distasteful. Old tobacco breath Herb, he calls him. She can't manage it alone and Harold, thankfully, accepts the indignity. He remains tight-lipped though, eyes closed. Herb used to attempt conversation but after his puppy dog overtures were consistently ignored, he focuses attention on Anne.

"Got a do over at the lodge," he says, after Harold is safely deposited in the canoe. "Starts around noon, so I probably won't be here when you get back."

Anne stares out at the water.

The first dark space melts away. Pure luck.

"Anyways," Herb continues, "seems like he's got so light, you should be able to manage him yourself."

Anne steadies the boat. "Thanks Herb," she says quickly, "I'll manage quite well." She concentrates on putting one foot and then the other into the canoe.

The day is perfect.

About a quarter of a mile down the bay, out a challenging swimming distance from the shore, the remnants of an old wooden diving dock lay submerged. She has no idea when it was in use but assumes by its deteriorated state, not for several decades, the fifties or sixties perhaps. She imagines a group of young cottage goers meeting here, boats and canoes tied to the bobbing dock, young men diving and showing off, women preening in the sun. Now most of it is a few feet below the surface with only one water-worn post as its beacon. Anne paddles steadily toward it.

She has arranged Harold so that his head is inclined upward resting on a life jacket positioned against the rear thwart. As soon as he is in the canoe and out from shore, his face always acquires a peaceful look, eyes half closed, thin lips slackened from their vigilant pursing. While still at the dock, Anne passingly thought of folding his arms across his chest but then Herb might have wondered.

She concentrates on the slap and pull of the paddle. Sun diamonds sparkle in the rippling water, the sea smell intoxicating. She hums a few lines.

"You're in a good mood," Harold says, opening his eyes to stare at her suspiciously.

"It's the day," she replies lightly. "Just look at it. The sky, the water. It's so warm."

"Been into the wine already?"

"Of course not. Would you like some?"

He nods.

She drags on the paddle and lets the canoe drift. They're in a calm spot and won't veer too far off course.

She can't remember when they've ever drunk wine from a bottle. It certainly wasn't Harold's style nor hers. She retrieves the bottle and unscrews the top. Even after one gulp, she feels slightly light-headed, younger.

Harold is thirsty and after five or six swigs, he belches loudly and closes his eyes.

The second dark space disappears. Wine and sun, perfect combo.

Anne paddles steadily toward the bobbing post. She thinks she remembers they paddled right over this sunken dock when they first discovered it several years ago. As the bow approaches the darkened form underwater, she hopes the dock hasn't heaved up in the interim, that the canoe bottom won't scrape or worse lodge itself in a rotted beam. She lifts the paddle and the craft drifts smoothly until it nudges gently into the protruding post.

Anne sits motionless staring at the post's grey water-worn surface. She has no idea how stable it is or whether it can bear her weight, even for a few moments. Quietly, she knots the painter as far down the post as she can reach. She doesn't want it to trip her. Harold mutters a few times and snorts. The sun is warmer now and small beads of sweat trickle down his forehead and onto his razor thin nose.

She wriggles gingerly out of her skirt and slips off her blouse, then leans back for a moment to let the sun's heat soak through her bathing suit. Such an ideal day for sunbathing. She unties the running shoes hanging from the picnic basket and fastens one on either side of the thin belt around the middle of her bathing suit. She twists back and forth a couple of times wondering how much they will drag.

Her clothes. She scrunches them into a ball intending to stow them in the bow then, impulsively, tosses first her skirt and then her blouse into the water. They balloon up and float momentarily until a series of choppy waves pull them under. Anne looks down at her out-of-style bathing suit. No turning back now.

When she tosses the towel over the post, the dolphins hang jauntily upside down, one on either side. The breeze slaps them lightly back and forth, their terry cloth faces stoically staring into the water. Anne turns around, back to Harold and eases herself up on the gunwales. The canoe rocks visibly. When Harold stirs, Anne is conscious of each hair on the back of her neck.

A gull screams out over the water. A small droplet of sweat runs down between her breasts. She concentrates on the dolphins and listens again for Harold. He's sound asleep, breathing like a baby.

The shoreline looks diminished, silent. She wonders if anyone is watching. She knows directly west of their house, there's a path that runs in a zig zag fashion from their property to the beach. She and Harold trekked down it once or twice after they were first married and more than once, she's seen surprised faces appear at the edge of their lawn only to disappear. Hikers probably thinking the trail led out to some road. There are no seaside cottages along this strip, but someone could easily hide in the trees. What would they think watching a full grown woman inch toward a towel-covered post; climb momentarily onto it; slip into the water? If she does it quickly and smoothly enough, they might only think they saw someone, a slight splash, a paddle hitting the water perhaps.

The entire process grinds into slow motion once she begins. Someone has turned on the timer and its tick accentuates her every move. She takes a deep breath and tries her weight against the post. It sways forward as her feet lose contact with the canoe gunwales. In a single motion, she rolls sideways and falls into the water with a loud splash. Her shoulder and hip hit slimy decaying wood underneath and the icy cold-water stings. She pushes away from the submerged dock and reappears a few feet from the canoe. Harold's sleeping face is silhouetted against the sky.

She pauses only a moment to whisper 'good luck' then her arms break into the familiar front crawl. She feels initially as though she is in a race and has to concentrate on keeping her pace moderate - it will be a long swim in, especially since it's her first time this summer in open sea water. At first she gasps every third stroke, feeling as though she can't breathe, then gradually relaxing a little, lets her arms pull her legs kick. Initially aware of the shoes dragging, she worries one or both will come loose, then forgets they are there, a mere rhythmical nudging with each stroke. Every time she turns her head to breathe, the sun warms her face. It's still so deep she can't see bottom but gradually rocks and submerged logs appear.

About halfway, she turns on her back for a much needed rest and floats for a few minutes, the sun reviving her stiffening limbs a little. When she flips back to continue, the shoreline still looks a long way off, trees and beach barely visible. One arm and then the other, her head says over and over as she settles back into the front crawl. Just keep going, eyes on the shore. Finally, the bottom comes into clear focus, small smooth pieces of driftwood and pebbles that gradually seem to rise to the surface. For the last few metres, she floats face down turning her head several times to catch her breath, arms out flat in front, letting the lapping waves wash her in. She's looking for a safe place to stand.

When her feet finally contact the rocky bottom she staggers, her breath in gasps. She steadies herself for a moment, in this thankfully warmer water then wills her legs to wade into shore. Her body is rapidly stiffening, and she must keep moving. She wades slowly up to the pebbled beach, a middle-aged mermaid emerging from the sea.

Anne finds a log and sits gingerly. Every muscle is beginning to ache. Her hands are numb and the running shoelaces slippery so the task of untying them from her belt is a challenge. She gets one but the other won't budge. She considers taking the belt off but then the lace would remain tied anyway. She's sure she can't jamb her foot in without loosening the laces. Panic tightens her throat, and she thinks she's going to cry. "Toughen up," she says aloud. "Try again." The second one finally gives, and she shakily manages to pull them on and tie the laces. When she stands, she feels momentarily light-headed. Her legs are full of lead, and she must force one in front of the next. She takes a final look toward the canoe, a mere bobbing dot on the horizon. As she trudges into the adjacent woods, she wonders when they find it, if they find the canoe, will they think she has drowned.

The trek through this scrub brush is more harrowing than she expected. The path she thought was there turns out to be overgrown and twice, she takes the wrong turn and has to back track. She is only vaguely conscious of her own body now; it's merely a transport device. Stones jab her feet through the shoes and branches scratch her legs and arms. She has turned off her nerve-endings; put them on hold.

The familiarity of the house roof momentarily weakens her resolve. She could still go back, make up some crazy alibi, get someone to row her out to him. No, she has no van here. She would have to walk or cycle to the dock and then what? She has made it this far. Recapitulation is not an option.

Once inside the back door, she pulls off her bathing suit and shoes and listens to the clock tick. Remnants of breakfast stare at her from the kitchen sink. She can't remember the last time she had stood alone in the house. And nude - never. She unbraids her hair and shakes it like a dog, sending a shower of water droplets onto the floor and kitchen furniture. She giggles at her own audacity and parades around the table once before entering the sun-filled dining room. The dark polished table *gleams invitingly. A long time ago in university, she briefly dated a photographer. He wanted her to pose nude and she wouldn't. Couldn't...*

She tries a couple of poses, sitting with one leg crossed over the other, then leans back on her arms like a sun bather. Her power point project is nearly complete. Only one dark space left - someone she knows could see her, either on the road or down at the ferry or both. Or not.

Out of the corner of her eye, the cardboard box on the mantle comes into focus, the dust inside, seeming to stare accusingly. Embarrassed, she jumps down.

After a quick shower, she dresses and closes her nap sack. Her hair is nearly dry, and she stands in front of the bedroom mirror brushing it, tossing it back and forth over her shoulders and brushing it again. She puts her wet bathing suit and the shoes into a garbage bag and stuffs them into the top of her nap sack. She'll dispose of them when she arrives at the ferry. It takes a few minutes to locate both postcards and, after placing them carefully into her wallet, crams it into the outside pocket of the nap sack. Just before she heads out, she remembers her Savings bank book, that she should have it with her just in case. It can't be found, of course, and she spends at least fifteen minutes hunting. Finally, when she dumps everything out of her purse onto her bed, there it is. She shoves it in beside her wallet.

Anne walks slowly toward the back door. None of it seems real now - what she has done, what she is about to do. It's almost as if she's watching someone else going through the motions, someone else preparing to leave.

Afternoon sunlight catches something shiny as Anne passes the side table. The silver dollar. She picks it up and carries it back to the mantle. Heads I win," she says softly, placing it on the cardboard lid. "Tails you lose."

She takes a last look back, the rooms and life she embraced twelve years ago; experiences a fleeting moment of regret before locking the door. She ignores her impending exhaustion and stiff legs as she wheels her bicycle from the shed. If she's lucky, she'll make the late afternoon ferry to the mainland.

The End